This book
belongs to

_____

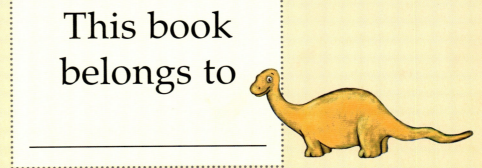

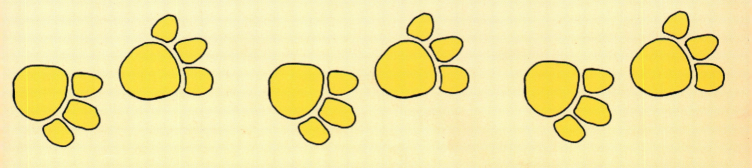

Desmond the Dinosaur Series

Desmond is Lonely
Desmond Starts School
Desmond Goes to the Vet
Desmond and the Monsters

HAPPY CAT BOOKS

Published by Happy Cat Books Ltd.
Bradfield, Essex CO11 2UT, UK

This edition published 2003
1 3 5 7 9 10 8 6 4 2

Text copyright © Althea Braithwaite 1989, 2003
Illustrations copyright © Sarah Wimperis, 2003
The moral rights of the author and illustrator have been asserted
All rights reserved

A CIP catalogue record for this book is available from the British Library

ISBN 1 903285 52 6 Paperback

Printed in Poland, DRUK INTRO SA

D ... to the Vet

Desmond

Desmond Dinosaur
3

Desmond Goes to the Vet

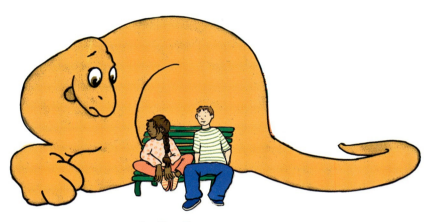

Althea

Illustrated by Sarah Wimperis

Happy Cat Books

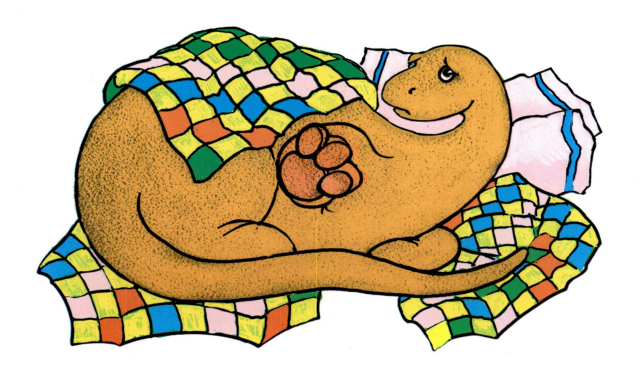

When Desmond got up one morning, he could
hardly walk. One of his legs hurt dreadfully.
It had been all right when he went to bed.

Desmond tried to get a close look, but he couldn't see anything wrong with his leg or his foot.

Desmond hobbled out to find his friends,
Joe and Selima.
"What's the matter Desmond,
why are you limping?"

Desmond said he didn't know, but it hurt.
His friends didn't know whether to take
Desmond to the doctor or the vet.

Desmond thought that the vet seemed better, because it was not so far to walk.

But when they got there, the
waiting room was very crowded.
There were lots of other animals.

They sat in the car park. It was a long wait.

Desmond was glad Joe and Selima had come
with him, because he would have been a bit
lonely and frightened waiting on his own.

The nurse called out to say, "The vet will see you now, Desmond."

First, the vet prodded at Desmond's leg.
"Ouch," said Desmond.
Then the vet used his torch to look into
Desmond's eyes.

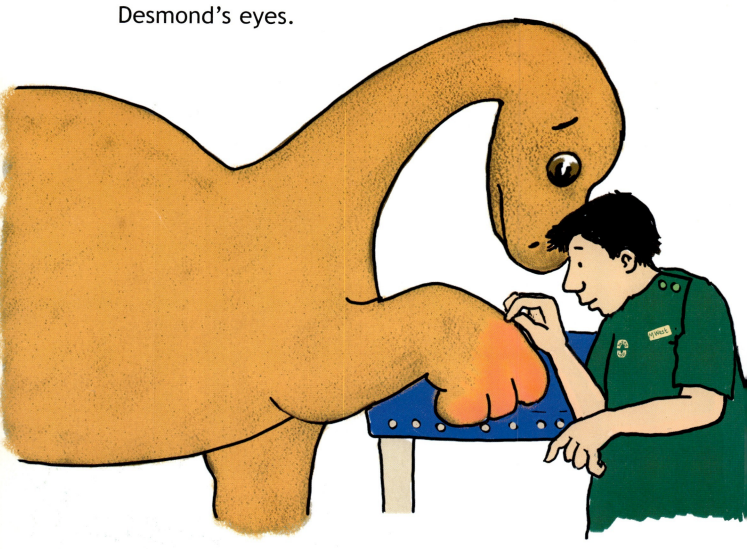

He asked Desmond to open his mouth to say "aah"! Desmond did as he was told, but he thought it was a bit odd, because it was his leg that hurt.

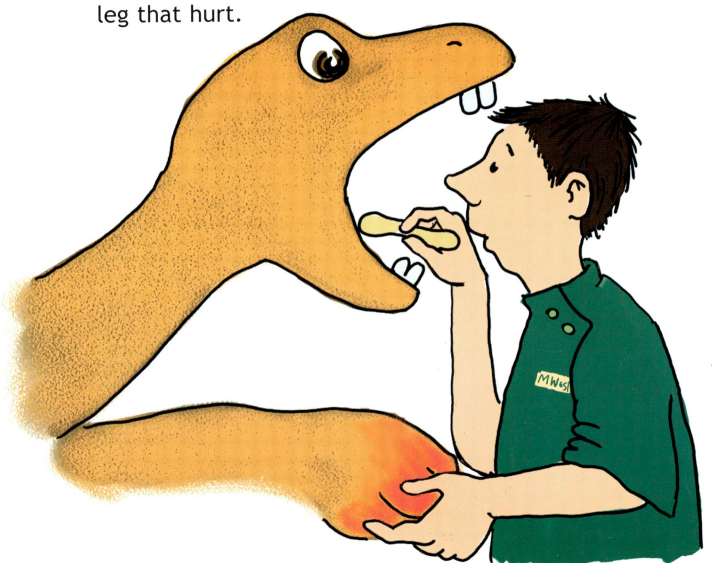

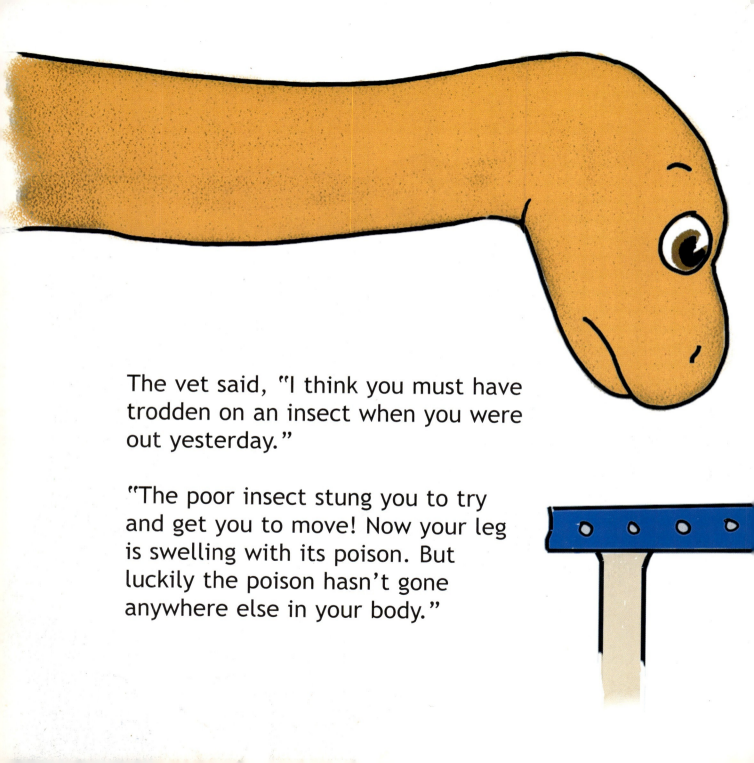

The vet said, "I think you must have trodden on an insect when you were out yesterday."

"The poor insect stung you to try and get you to move! Now your leg is swelling with its poison. But luckily the poison hasn't gone anywhere else in your body."

The vet filled a large syringe with medicine. "I am going to inject this medicine into your leg to make the poison go away."

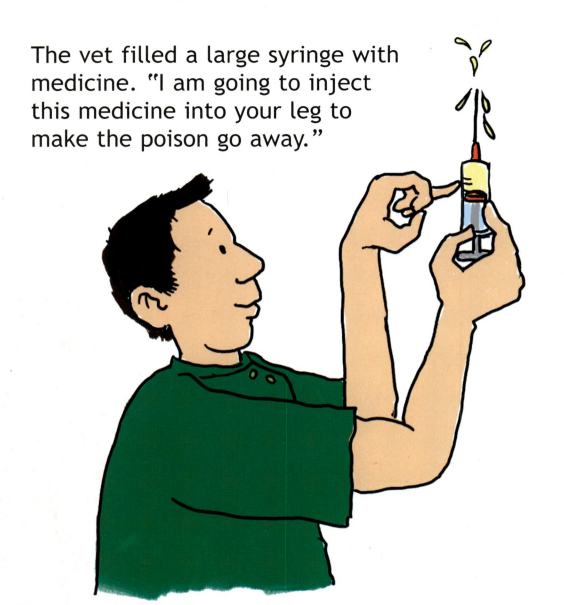

"It will hurt as it goes in, but it will make your leg better."

Desmond felt nervous, but Joe stroked him and said, "It doesn't hurt much, I've had it done to me."

Soon it was over and Desmond agreed it hadn't hurt much.

The vet put a plaster on Desmond's leg, just to make sure no dirt could get in.

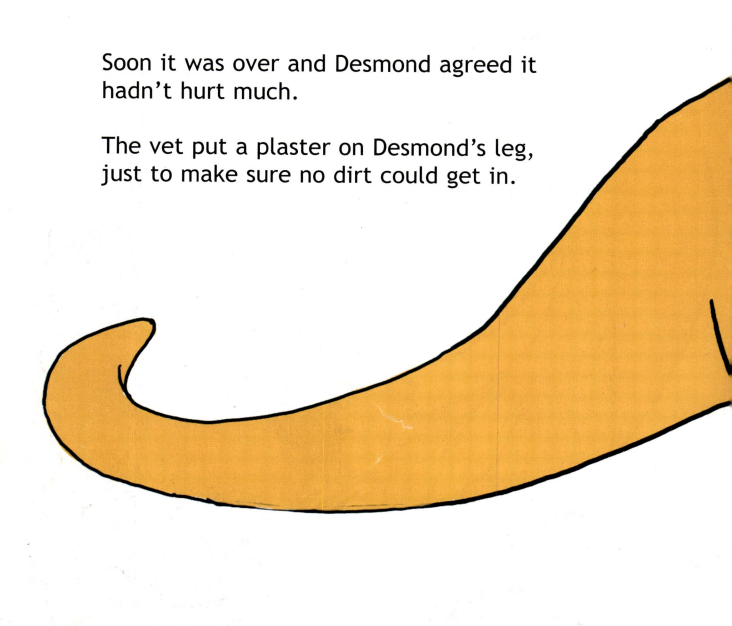

The vet told Desmond to go home and rest.
"Come back and see me, if it's not better tomorrow."

Desmond thanked the vet and limped off home.
Joe and Selima went with him.

Selima sat and read to Desmond
as he slowly fell asleep.

When Desmond woke up next morning he felt much better. He could walk on all four legs again.

"I hope the insect feels better too," he thought.